STEPHEN E. FABIAN'S
Ladies & Legends

STEPHEN E. FABIAN'S
Ladies & Legends

UNDERWOOD-MILLER
Novato, California
Lancaster, Pennsylvania

STEPHEN E. FABIAN'S LADIES AND LEGENDS
ISBN 0-88733-167-X (Softcover Edition)
ISBN 0-88733-168-8 (Cloth Edition)

Library of Congress Cataloging-in-Publication Data
Fabian, Stephen E.
     [Ladies and Legends]
     Stephen E. Fabian's ladies and legends.
          p.   cm.
     ISBN 0-88733-168-8 (cloth edition) : $24.95. -- ISBN 0-88733-167-X (softcover edition) :
$14.95
          1. Fabian, Stephen E., 1930— –Themes, motives. 2. Science ficiton—illustrations.   I. Title.
II. Title: Ladies and legends
     NC975.5.F25A4 1993
     741.6'092 — dc20   92-28142
                                                                                 CIP

INTRODUCTION

One of the luminaries in the firmament of American fantasy illustrators is Stephen E. Fabian, a versatile artist compared by some with the fantasy masters, Virgil Finlay and Hannes Bok.

But the label "another Finlay" or "the new Bok" is neither accurate nor fair. While Fabian has proved to be a maestro of many techniques, his most frequent and familiar style is unique to him and not to be likened to any other art in the field.

Stephen E. Fabian came late to professional illustration. Whereas most of our leading artists in the field, began drawing in their teens and were appearing professionally in their twenties, Steve waited until the age of 37 to have his first piece of work published. He did not appear in the pages of a professional science fiction magazine until 1974. He was 44 at that time.

Despite his late start, Fabian has already been nominated for the Hugo as best artist at the World Science Fiction Convention and for best artist the first World Fantasy Convention held in Providence, R.I.

Stephen E. Fabian was born in Garfield, N.J., on January 3, 1930. He was raised and attended school in nearby Passaic. While serving as a Facsimile instructor in the U.S. Air Force at Scott A.F.B. in Illinois in 1950, Fabian discovered magazine science fiction and was captivated by the works of such authors as Isaac Asimov, Ray Bradbury, Robert A. Heinlein, Clifford Simak and Theodore Sturgeon. While he enjoyed reading science fiction, he was also fascinated by the cover paintings and interior illustrations of Bok, Finlay and Edd Cartier.

He was married in 1955 and his wife, Dorothy, bore him two sons, Stephen Jr. and Andy.

In 1965 the Fabians left New Jersey for Middlebury, Vermont, when Steve gained a position with Simmons Precision, Inc. While in Vermont Steve began doing drawings for fan magazines, and his first published effort was a 1967 cover for *Twilight Zine*. Although long a fan of fantasy art, he did not find turning his enthusiasm into actual drawings a simple task. He worked hard, without formal art training, and gradually the long hours of labor paid off.

A major decision in his life came early in 1974, when the nationwide slump in the aerospace industry resulted in his being laid off. Steve was faced with a choice of seeking other employment in the engineering line or pursuing his new art career full time. He chose art.

In 1974 Fabian already had quite a few credits to show for his seven years as a part-time artist. The trick was to crack the pro ranks, and this he did with a black and white drawing in the August, 1974 issue of *Galaxy Science Fiction*.

He soon became a familiar figure in such magazines as *If, Galaxy, Amazing, Fantastic,* and *Isaac Asimov's Science Fiction Magazine*, doing interiors and covers.

His first book illustration was in 1973 for THE FIREFIEND AND THE RAVEN by Charles Gardette and Edgar Allan Poe. Since then he has illustrated books for numerous publishers including the Doubleday Science Fiction Book Club, Underwood-Miller, Donald Grant, Paul Ganley, Oswald Train, Houghton-Mifflin, Arkham House, Wildside Press, Owlswick Press, Phantasia Press, and others.

For the paperback market Fabian has taken assignments from Avon, Ace, Zebra, Donning, Pyramid, and TSR, Inc.

Late in 1975, the Fabians moved back to NJ where Steve, with the assistance of his wife Dot continues to work on current book and magazine assignments.

Gerry de la Ree
1924-1993

STEPHEN E. FABIAN'S
Ladies & Legends

THE DRAGON OF THE ISHTAR GATE by L. Sprague de Camp (1982) (front cover painting)

Fantasy illustration

Fantasy illustration

Bellerophon

Private commission for Loci Lenar (1985)

Fantasy illustration

Among those whom Vermoulian had called forth was the graceful Mersei

from RHIALTO THE MARVELLOUS by Jack Vance (1984)

One day at idle whim Rhialto built a sand-castle on the beach

from RHIALTO THE MARVELLOUS by Jack Vance (1984)

"I come in Lord Asteroth's stead," boomed the awful voice

from RAUM by Carl Sherrell (1977)

His other arm was raised high, ax in hand

from RAUM by Carl Sherrell (1977)

Price's fist crashed against Ali's jaw

from GOLDEN BLOOD by Jack Williamson (1982)

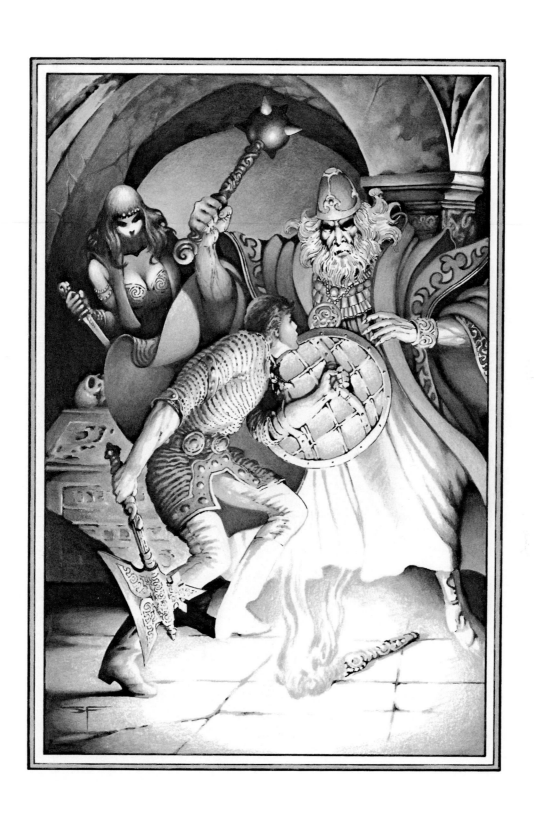

Malikar leapt into the tomb

from GOLDEN BLOOD by Jack Williamson (1982)

The battle in the garden

from GUINEVERE AND LANCELOT & OTHERS by Arthur Machen (1986)

The castle of Sir Sagramour

from GUINEVERE AND LANCELOT & OTHERS by Arthur Machen (1986)

The seventeen virgins

from CUGEL'S SAGA by Jack Vance (1983)

The Rat Cave
....
from THE EYES OF THE OVERWORLD by Jack Vance (1977)

The Iron Coach

from GUINEVERE AND LANCELOT & OTHERS by Arthur Machen (1986)

The Incantation

from GUINEVERE AND LANCELOT & OTHERS by Arthur Machen (1986)

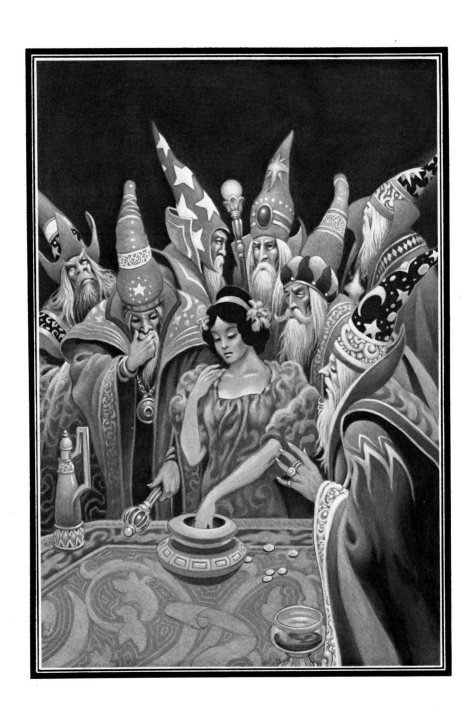

You must reach into the pot, thoroughly stir the chips, and bring forth one

from RHIALTO THE MARVELLOUS by Jack Vance (1984)

The semblance of Calanctus took form on the worktable

from RHIALTO THE MARVELLOUS by Jack Vance (1984)

A hairy, black horror swung past him with a clashing of frothing fangs

from Conan: *The Tower of the Elephant* (Portfolio, 1977)

Red Sonya (from "The Shadow of the Vulture" by Robert E. Howard)

from *Fantastic Nudes* (Portfolio, 1976–First Series)

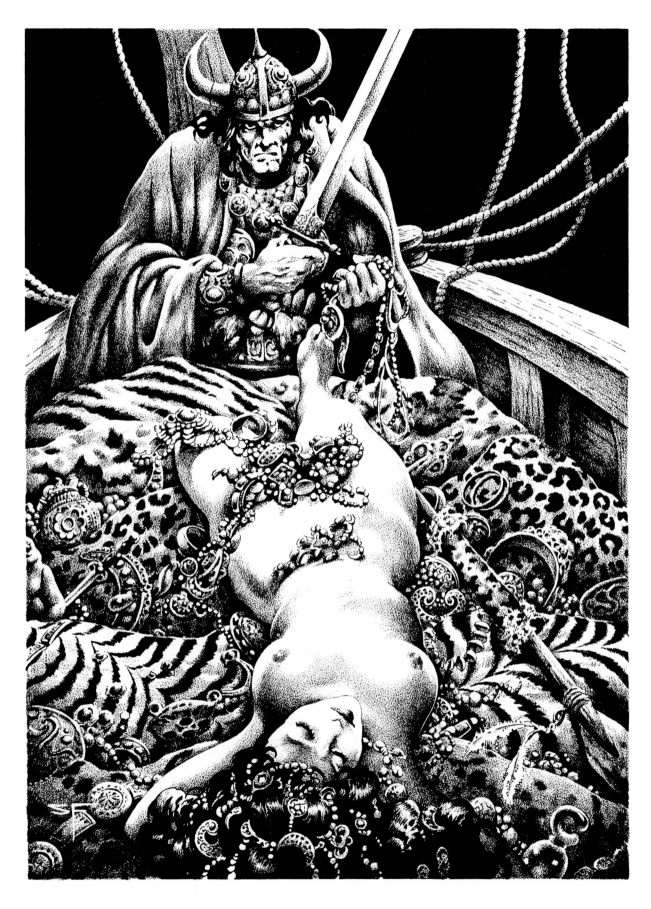

Like a true queen she lay, with her plunder heaped high about her

from *Conan: Queen of the Black Coast* (Portfolio, 1976)

Duare (from PIRATES OF VENUS by E. R. Burroughs)

from *Fantastic Nudes* (Portfolio, 1976–Second Series)

from "A Letter from God" by Ian Watson

He uncovered twelve men and five women ...

from FOR A BREATH I TARRY by Roger Zelazny (1980)

Four or five of the prospects and initiates were begging for their lives

from CARNIFEX MARDI GRAS by John F. Carr (1982)

from CARNIFEX MARDI GRAS by John F. Carr (1982)

He pointed his finger; a flicker of emotion spurted forth to shatter a boulder

from MORREION by Jack Vance (1979)

He cast a spell of buoyancy upon the palace

from MORREION by Jack Vance (1979)

Zaraide's Dwelling

from THE EYES OF THE OVERWORLD by Jack Vance (1977)

The Laughing Magician's Manse

from THE EYES OF THE OVERWORLD by Jack Vance (1977)

Price saw it was a bleached human skull

from GOLDEN BLOOD by Jack Williamson (1982)

Price rode down into the wadi

from GOLDEN BLOOD by Jack Williamson (1982)

Vekyra

from GOLDEN BLOOD by Jack Williamson (1982)

She wrapped the cloak about his shoulders

from GOLDEN BLOOD by Jack Williamson (1982)

They seemed like creatures trained to hide and hunt

from "The Pedlar of Pendle," THE SCALLION STONE by Canon Basil A. Smith (1980)

A fleeting glimpse showed the giant tawny shape, rearing upright against the stars ...

from Conan: *The Tower of the Elephant* (Portfolio, 1977)

Flowers were tangled in her hair

from WE ARE ALL LEGENDS by Darrell Schweitzer (1981)

Ephemeral towers and embattlements and gates flickered like mirages in a desert.

from WE ARE ALL LEGENDS by Darrell Schweitzer (1981)

from BORN TO EXILE by Phyllis Eisenstein

from ALIEN FLESH by Seabury Quinn

The ghostly city

from THE EYES OF THE OVERWORLD by Jack Vance (1977)

"What intricate effort is this?"

from THE EYES OF THE OVERWORLD by Jack Vance (1977)

"They wanted me, oh how they wanted me."

from "Scape-Goats" by Clive Barker

"Once every generation or so, the desert spat out its demons."

from "The Skins of the Fathers" by Clive Barker

from THE RETURN OF THE SEA-FARER by Robert E. Howard

He scooped the mermaid up before she even had time to bite.

from ANITA by Keith Roberts (1990)

from "Locksley Hall-2025 A.D." by G.H. Stine

The Missionaries

from *The Science Fiction Review*

The Demon Encounter

from THE EYES OF THE OVERWORLD by Jack Vance (1977)

On closer inspection Cugel saw a prodigious mound of gelatinous flesh

from CUGEL'S SAGA by Jack Vance (1979)

from THE COMPLEAT CROW by Brian Lumley (1987)

In the air he shaped a figure with a forefinger

from "The Lord of the Worms," THE COMPLEAT CROW by Brian Lumley (1987)

I stood on Crow's doorstep and banged upon his heavy oak door

from "Name and Number," THE COMPLEAT CROW by Brian Lumley (1987)

Titus Crow in Study (cover painting)

from THE COMPLEAT CROW by Brian Lumley (1987)

"Take your allotted glass–and face your hostess."

from "The Wine-Glasses at Hagthwaite Hall," by Canon Basil A. Smith (1980)

He whirled, the blade's naked steel glistening ...

from THE DEVIL'S AUCTION by Robert Weinberg (1988)

"William 'Billy' Fovargue–accused of wizardry–was hanged on that tree in 1675

from "Billy's Oak," THE COMPLEAT CROW by Brian Lumley (1987)

from *Weirdbook*

from "Sex, Death & Starshine" by Clive Barker

from "New Murders in the Rue Morgue" by Clive Barker

from TWILIGHT RIVER

from TWILIGHT RIVER

from *Conan: The Tower of the Elephant* (Portfolio, 1976)

from THE WHITE ISLE by Darrell Schweitzer (1989)

Then the crowd closed in

from "Rawhead Rex" by Clive Barker

The masterpiece ... tottered and then–it began to fall

from "In the Hills, the Cities" by Clive Barker

"After him!" bawled Ildefonse. "He must not escape!"

from MORREION by Jack Vance (1979)

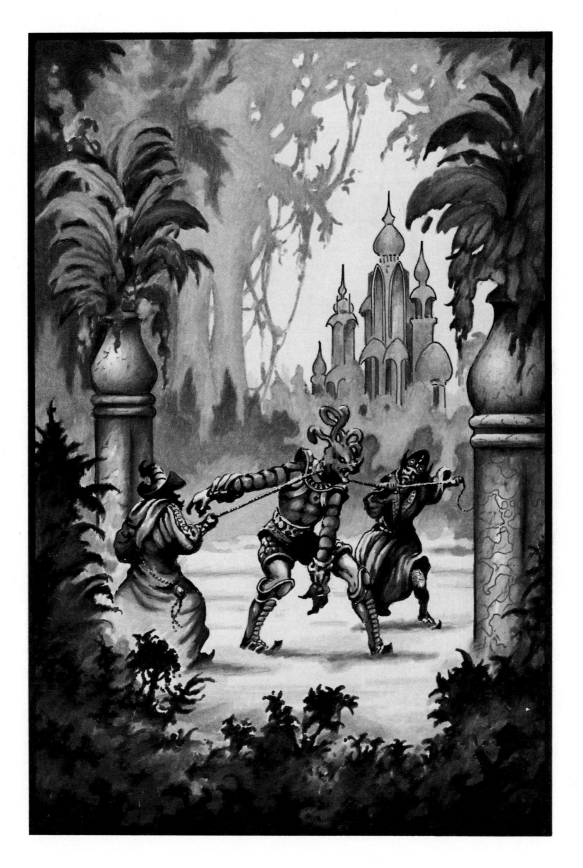

Flinging a pair of nooses about the supple neck, they held him

from MORREION by Jack Vance (1979)

Retreat of the rat-folk

from THE EYES OF THE OVERWORLD by Jack Vance (1977)

A ghost appeared

from THE EYES OF THE OVERWORLD by Jack Vance (1977)

The bird-women set up an alarm

from RHIALTO THE MARVELLOUS by Jack Vance (1984)

He watched his elite knights on their flyers darting down upon the war-wagons

from RHIALTO THE MARVELLOUS by Jack Vance (1984)

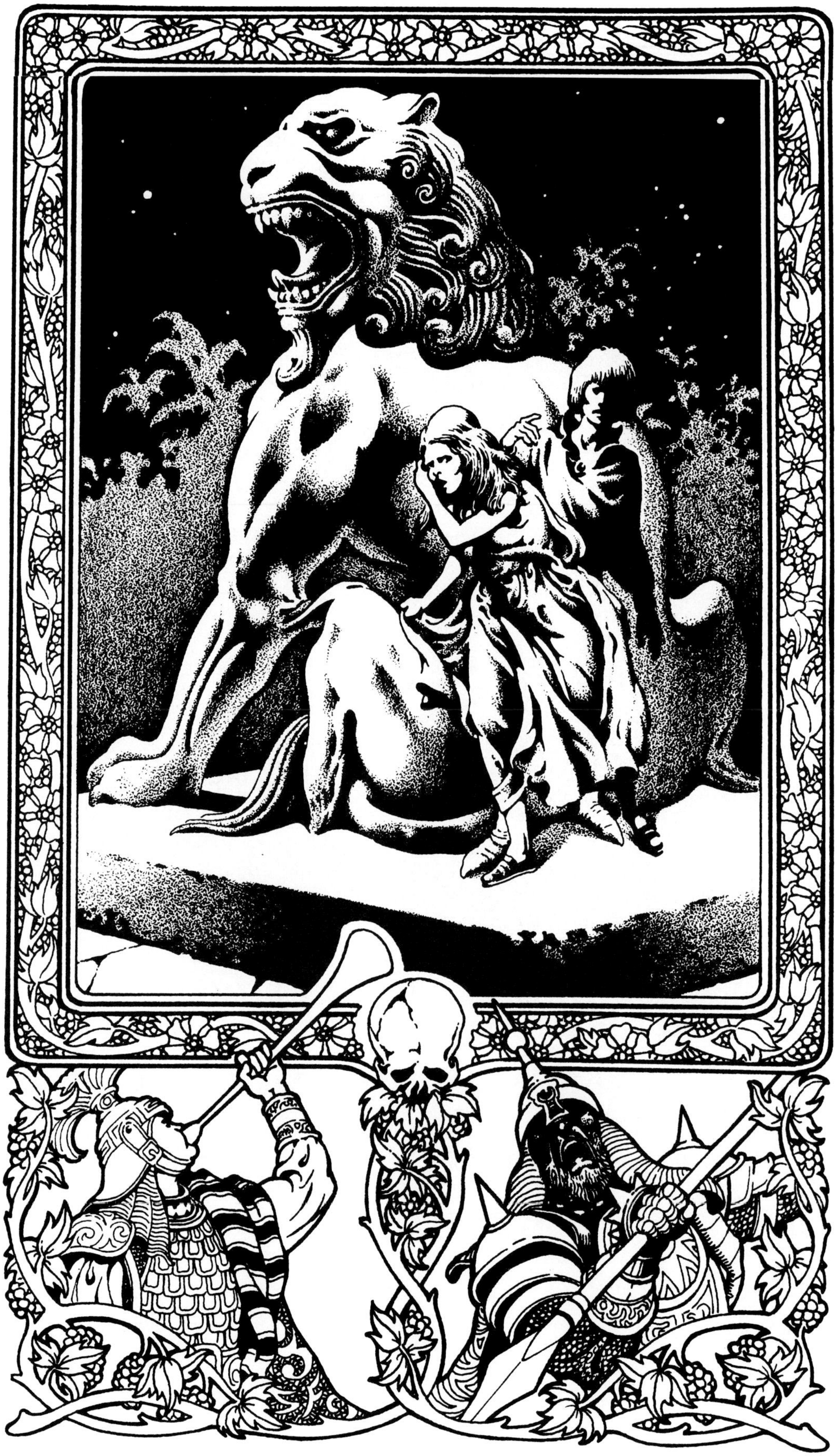

Black & white illustration

Black & white illustration

He stared at the mummied skull, which grinned back at him

from "A-mazed in Oriab," ICED ON ARAN & OTHER DREAM QUESTS by Brian Lumley (1992)

Whatever she saw, it robbed her of her senses

from "Augeren," ICED ON ARAN & OTHER DREAM QUESTS by Brian Lumley (1992)

She did not stop for any great last thoughts but walked steadily into the water ...

from ANITA by Keith Roberts (1990)

from "The Story of the Brown Man," TOM O'BEDLAM'S NIGHT OUT by Darrell Schweitzer (1985)

from ANITA by Keith Roberts (1990)

Then a flicker of light from the campfire showed outline of a club falling toward his head

from CARNIFEX MARDI GRAS by John F. Carr (1982)

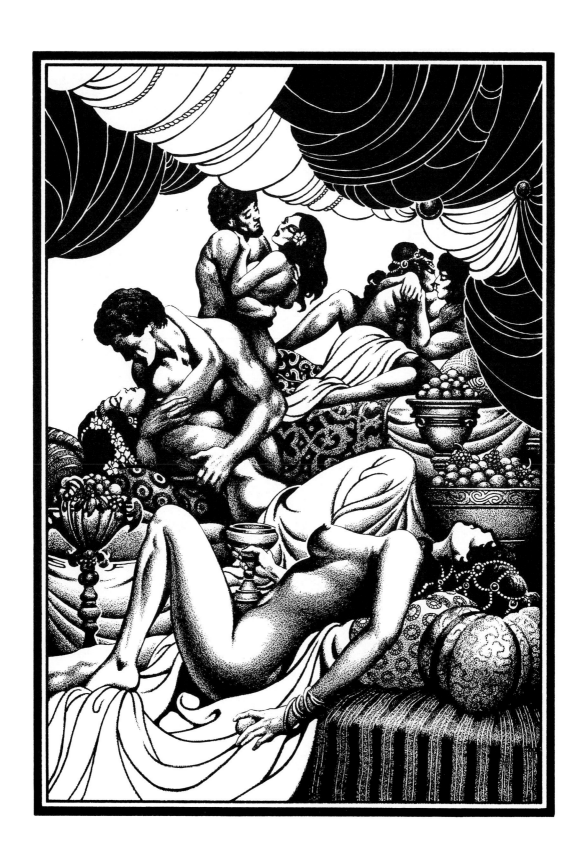

from "Afterglow" by Arthur Machen

from "A Vision of Rembathene," TOM O'BEDLAM'S NIGHT OUT by Darrell Schweitzer (1985)

... his back against the mast, he heaped mangled corpses at his feet ...

from Conan: *Queen of the Black Coast* (Portfolio, 1977)

Holding the still-pulsing organ over the blazing jewel, a rain of blood fell on the stone!

from *Conan: The Tower of the Elephant* (Portfolio, 1976)

... he saw the gleaming tower crash into shining shards

from *Conan: The Tower of the Elephant* (Portfolio, 1976)

The image had the body of a man, but the head was one of nightmare and madness ...

from Conan: The Tower of the Elephant (Portfolio, 1976)

from DAUGHTER OF THE BRIGHT MOON by Lynn Abbey

from DAUGHTER OF THE BRIGHT MOON by Lynn Abbey

from "After the Last Elf is Dead" by Harry Turtledove, *Weird Tales*, (1988)

from "De Marigny's Clock," THE COMPLEAT CROW by Brian Lumley (1987)

from "A Lantern Maker of Ai Hanlo," by Darrell Schweitzer (1985)

from "The Story of Dadar," by Darrell Schweitzer (1985)

from "Tom O'Bedlam's Night Out," by Darrell Schweitzer (1985)

from "The Last Child of Masferigon," by Darrell Schweitzer (1985)

Osherl split the pen into a million motes

from RHIALTO THE MARVELLOUS by Jack Vance (1984)

Llorio spoke a spell of twisting and torsion, but Calanctus fended it away

from RHIALTO THE MARVELLOUS by Jack Vance (1984)

from DAUGHTER OF THE BRIGHT MOON by Lynn Abbey

from "Met Gelijke Munt" by C.A. Cador

"They are hidden under the floorboards of my cottage," said Xexamedes in a sulky voice

from RHIALTO THE MARVELLOUS by Jack Vance (1984)

"I must withhold my testimony until I am guaranteed fairly my life."

from RHIALTO THE MARVELLOUS by Jack Vance (1984)

The White Witch Llorio dominated all

from RHIALTO THE MARVELLOUS by Jack Vance (1984)

Vermoulian cast a spell of buoyancy upon the palace

from RHIALTO THE MARVELLOUS by Jack Vance (1984)

The roof glowed a vivid orange and melted to spawn a thousand symbols

from MORREION by Jack Vance (1979)

Ildefonse summoned one of his maidens

from MORREION by Jack Vance (1979)

The monastic ruins

from ''The Propert Bequest,'' THE SCALLION STONE by Canon Basil A. Smith (1980)

"It's more of a geological curio–something between an oblong block and a wedge."

from "The Scallion Stone," THE SCALLION STONE, Canon Basil A. Smith (1980)

"It is the cobra goddess Mertseger, who guards the tombs of the dead."

from THE DRAGON OF THE ISHTAR GATE by L. Sprague de Camp (1982)

The monster rose to his hindlegs.

from THE DRAGON OF THE ISHTAR GATE by L. Sprague de Camp (1982)

Steel flashed and the throng surged wildy back ...

from Conan: *The Tower of the Elephant* (Portfolio, 1976)

"Better we had cut our throats than come to this place. It is haunted."

from Conan: *The Tower of the Elephant* (Portfolio, 1976)

from "Confessions of a (Pornographer's) Shroud" by Clive Barker

from "Son of Celluloid" by Clive Barker

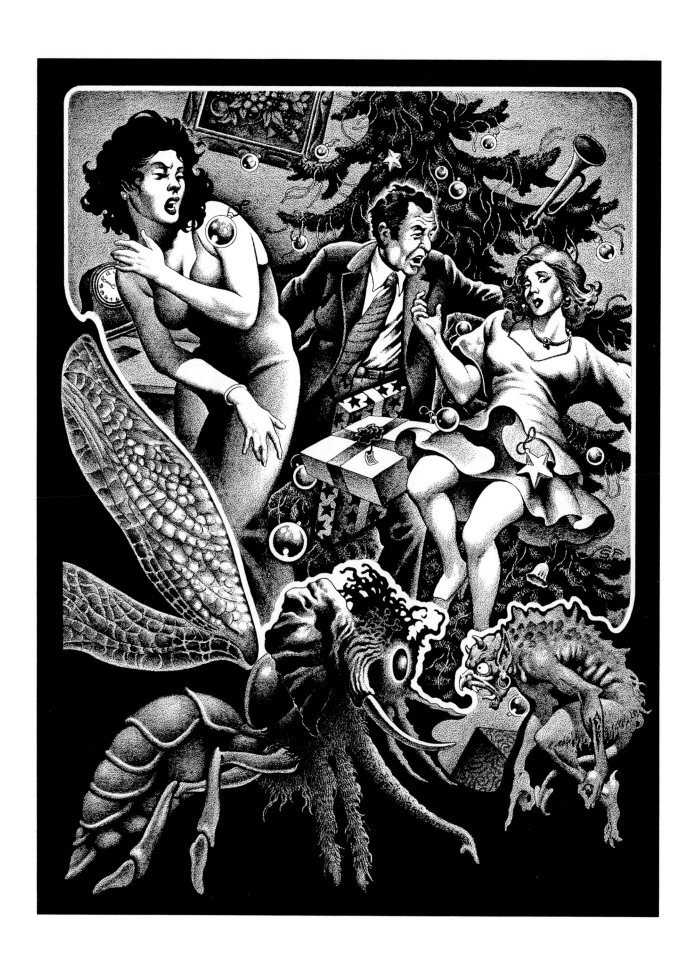

from "The Yattering & Jack" by Clive Barker

from "The Book of Blood" by Clive Barker

Sir John put his arm round her. "Look, look at the stars."

from ANITA by Keith Roberts (1990)

from *Science Fiction Review*

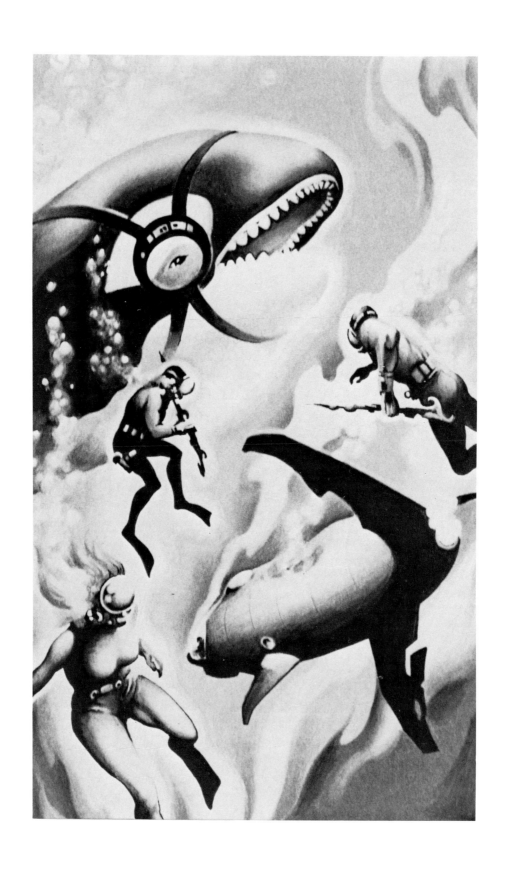

Now the Hunter ship was fluttering down out of sight

from THE SPACE SWIMMERS by Gordon R. Dickson (1979)

The Risso's dolphin fled. The sea leopard followed close.

from THE SPACE SWIMMERS by Gordon R. Dickson (1979)

Around all the battleground drifted strange fish of the lower deep

from THE SPACE SWIMMERS by Gordon R. Dickson (1979)

The looming, uprising silver-black peaks of undersea mountains

from THE SPACE SWIMMERS by Gordon R. Dickson (1979)

Ayesha (from SHE by H. R. Haggard)

from *Fantastic Nudes* (Portfolio, 1977–Second Series)

The White Sybil of Polarion (from "The White Sybil" by Clark Ashton Smith)

from *Fantastic Nudes* (Portfolio, 1977–First Series)

He climbed to the crest of a dune and looked in all directions

from CUGEL's SAGA by Jack Vance (1983)

The Galante

from CUGEL's SAGA by Jack Vance (1983)

Fantasy illustration

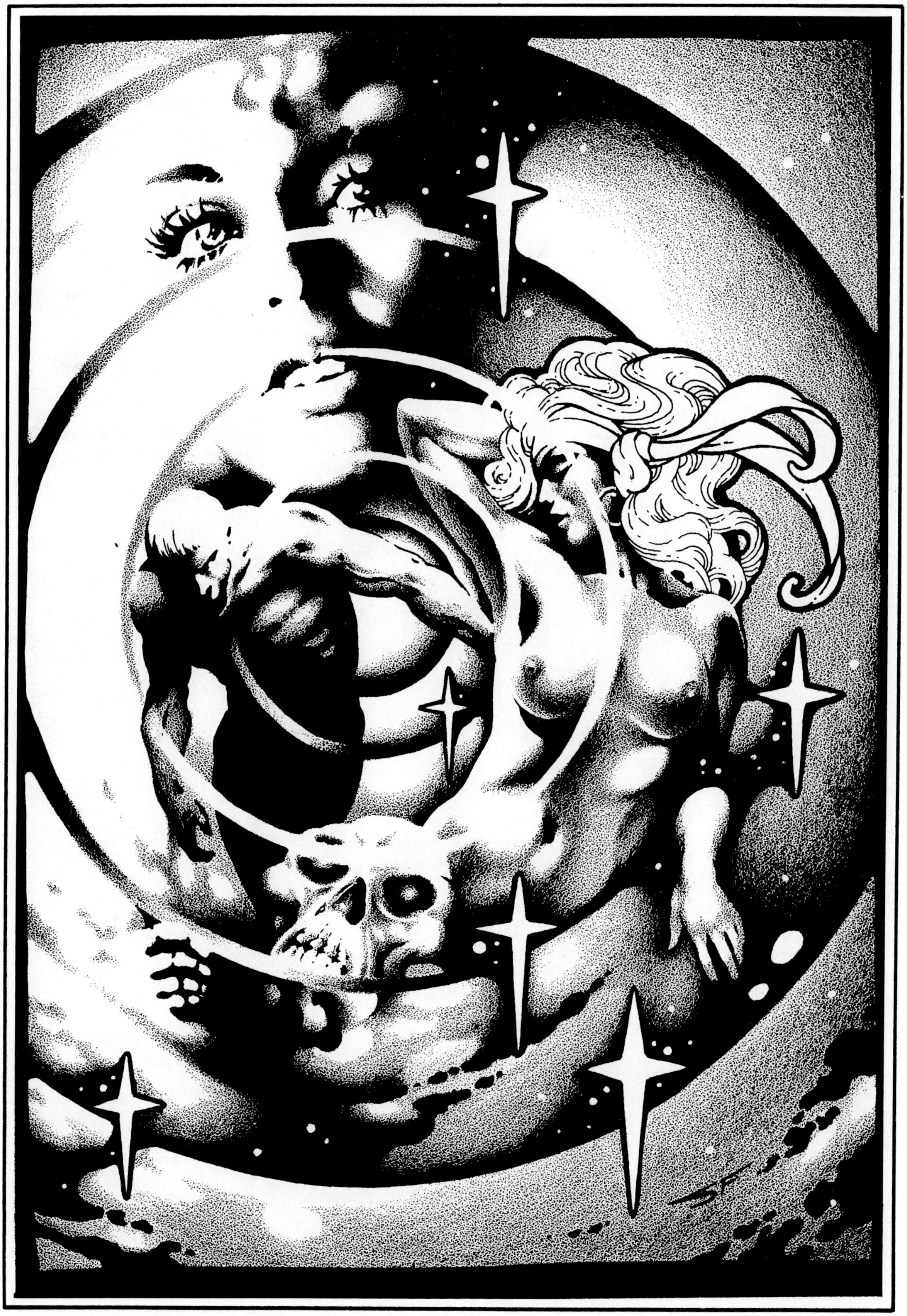

Fantasy illustration

In one mad instant she was there–vibrant with love fierce as a she-panther's

from *Conan: Queen of the Black Coast* (Portfolio, 1977)

Then the rest were on him in a nightmare rush of blazing eyes and dripping fangs

from *Conan: Queen of the Black Coast* (Portfolio, 1977)

"Wolves of the blue sea, behold ye now the dance–the mating-dance of Bêlit ..."

from *Conan: Queen of the Black Coast* (Portfolio, 1977)

She belonged to the sea; to its everlasting mystery he returned her

from *Conan: Queen of the Black Coast* (Portfolio, 1977)

Lur (from DWELLERS IN THE MIRAGE by A. Merritt)

from *Fantastic Nudes* (Portfolio, 1976–First Series)

The raft

from THE EYES OF THE OVERWORLD by Jack Vance (1977)

Fader's Waft (title page)

from RHIALTO THE MARVELLOUS by Jack Vance (1984)

Morreion (title page)

from RHIALTO THE MARVELLOUS by Jack Vance (1984)

from Conan: *Queen of the Black Coast* (Portfolio, 1977)